Finn and the
Leprechaun's Gold

For Fynn, Oscar, Sage, Olivia and Frances – MG

First published in 2008
by Wayland

This paperback edition published in 2009

Wayland
338 Euston Road
London NW1 3BH

Wayland Australia
Level 17/207 Kent Street
Sydney, NSW 2000

Series Editor: Louise John
Editor: Katie Powell
Cover design: Paul Cherrill
Design: D.R.ink
Consultant: Shirley Bickler

A CIP catalogue record for this book is available from the British Library.

ISBN 9780750254724 (hbk)
ISBN 9780750254731 (pbk)

Printed in China

Wayland is a division of Hachette Children's Books,
an Hachette Livre UK company

www.hachettelivre.co.uk

Finn and the Leprechaun's Gold

Written by Mick Gowar
Illustrated by Tim Archbold

WAYLAND

"Good morning, Finn," called Jim the Carter. "Why are you out walking in the rain?"

"I'm going to Galway City," said Finn. "I'm off to seek my fortune."

"That's where I'm going," said Jim. "Climb up and I'll give you a lift."

The rain slowed and the sun began to shine. A rainbow appeared in the sky.

"Stop the cart!" shouted Finn. "It's a rainbow. Everyone knows leprechauns hide gold at the end of the rainbow!"

Finn jumped off the cart and ran towards the rainbow.

He ran over fields...

...through sharp thorn hedges

...and across peat bogs.

Finn had almost reached the end of the rainbow when he heard a small voice. "Help! Can anyone hear me? Heeeeelp!"

"Where are you?" called Finn.

"I'm down here," cried the little voice at the bottom of the well. Finn peered into the well. "Don't worry," he said. "I'll get you out."

"Have you got a rope?" called the
little voice.

"No," said Finn, "but I've got a pair
of braces."

Finn took off his braces and hung them down the well.

"I can't quite reach them," cried the little man.

"Don't worry," said Finn. "I've got a tie, too." Finn tied his tie to the braces.

"I still can't reach," said the little man.

"Don't worry," said Finn. "I've also got a hanky." Finn tied his hanky to the tie.

"I still can't reach," said the little man.

So Finn tied his socks to the hanky.
"Got it!" shouted the little man.

Finn pulled on the home-made rope. It felt like someone very heavy was on the end, but it was only a tiny leprechaun.

"Thank you for saving me," said the leprechaun. "I was running to hide my purseful of gold at the end of the rainbow, but I fell into the well. To thank you for helping me, I'll give you one wish."

"I wish I had your purse in my hand right now!" said Finn.

"Easy!" cried the leprechaun. He clapped his hands and there was a puff of smoke.

Finn opened his eyes. He was at the bottom of the well. He was holding a large empty leather purse.

"I forgot to tell you," laughed the leprechaun. "I took all the gold out of my purse and put it in my hat before you pulled me out of the well! Goodbye!"

And he vanished.

"Help!" shouted Finn.

"Is that you, Finn?" asked Jim
the Carter.

"Yes," shouted Finn. "Can you pull me out?"

"I haven't got a rope," shouted Jim, "but some fool left his braces, his tie, his socks and his handkerchief all tied together. I'll use that."

Jim hung the home-made rope down the well and Finn climbed out.

"Who would be silly enough to tie his braces, his tie, his hanky and his socks together and leave them here?" asked Jim.

Finn put his hands in his pockets to hold his trousers up. He looked down at his bare feet. "It must have been someone really, really silly," he agreed.

And Jim the Carter laughed all the way home.

START READING is a series of highly enjoyable books for beginner readers. **The books have been carefully graded to match the Book Bands widely used in schools.** This enables readers to be sure they choose books that match their own reading ability.

Look out for the Band colour on the book in our Start Reading logo.

The Bands are:

	Pink Band 1
	Red Band 2
	Yellow Band 3
	Blue Band 4
	Green Band 5
	Orange Band 6
	Turquoise Band 7
	Purple Band 8
	Gold Band 9

START READING books can be read independently or shared with an adult. They promote the enjoyment of reading through satisfying stories supported by fun illustrations.

Mick Gowar has written more than 70 books for children, and likes to visit schools and libraries to give readings and lead workshops. He has also written plays and songs, and has worked with many orchestras. Mick writes his books in a shed in Cambridge.

Tim Archbold believes that making your fortune can be a difficult thing to do. Grumpy kings are hard to please, magic goats are always difficult to work with and the end of a rainbow is just over the next hill. But keep trying and have some fun on the way to your fortune...